First published in hardback in Great Britain by Andersen Press Ltd in 1993
First published in paperback by Picture Lions in 1994
This edition published by Collins Picture Books in 2001

1 3 5 7 9 10 8 6 4 2
ISBN: 0-00-776794-3

Picture Lions and Collins Picture Books are imprints of the Children's Division, part of HarperCollins Publishers Ltd.

Text and illustrations copyright © Tony Ross 1993, 2001

The author/illustrator asserts the moral right to be identified as the author/illustrator of the work.

A CIP catalogue record for this title is available from the British Library.

Visit our website at: www.harpercollinschildrensbooks.co.uk

Printed in Thailand

I Want To Be

Tony Ross

HarperCollins *Children's Books*

"The time has come to grow up," thought the little princess.

"I wonder how I should do it? Perhaps I should be different."

"But what sort of different should I be?"

"That's not what I should be. I'd better ask Mum."

"What is the best way to be?" she asked.
"Be kind…" said her mother,

"…like your father."

"What is the best way to be?" the little princess asked.
"Be loving," said her father,

"…like your mother."

"What is the best way to be?" the little princess asked.
"Be clean," said the cook.

"There is such a lot to remember," thought the little princess.
"I must be kind, loving and clean."

"What is the best way to be?" the little princess asked.
"Be brave," said the general.

"Be brave," thought the little princess.
"That's it! Then I could get spiders out of the bath myself."

"What is the best way to be?" the little princess asked.
"Be good at swimming..." said the admiral,

"...then you will be safe if your boat ever sinks."

"What is the best way to be?" the little princess asked.
"Be clever," said the prime minister.

"And be healthy," said the doctor.

"Oh dear!" thought the little princess. "I must be kind, loving and clean, brave, good at swimming, clever and healthy. I haven't got that many fingers!"

"Growing up is SO difficult."

"What is the best way to be?" asked the little princess.
"Oh, I don't know," said the maid.

"I suppose the important question is… what do YOU want to be?"

"I want to be..."

"TALL," said the little princess.

"But you ARE tall," said the little prince.

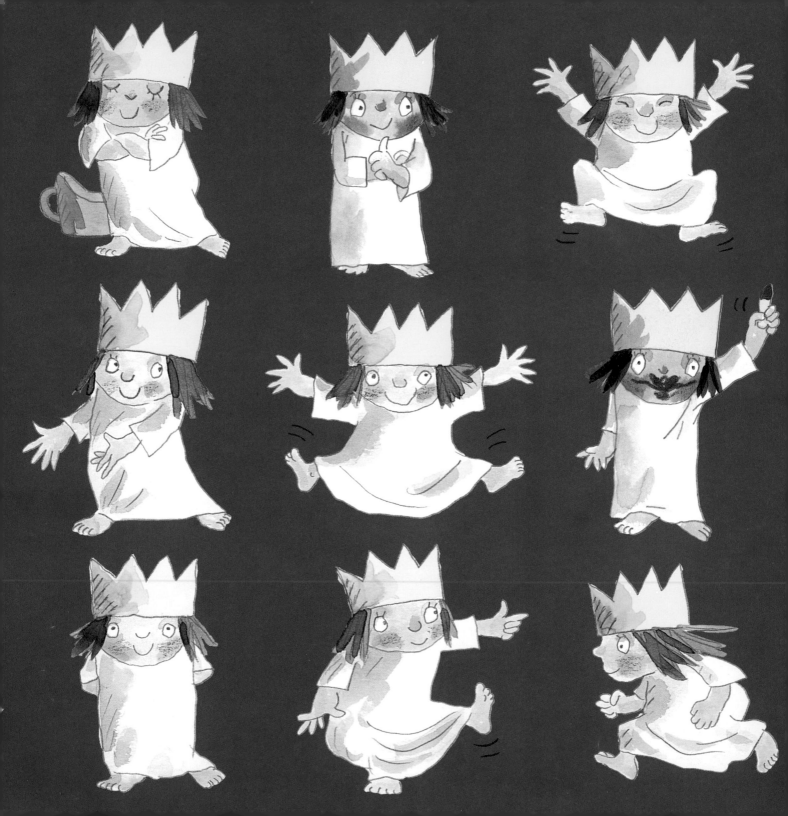